The Raven's Nest

MUD

ISBN: 978-0-9858838-8-1

DEDICATION

This is dedicated to my brothers Austin, Chris, Christian, Cameron, Zach, Logan, Kieran, Harvinder, Phillip, Marcus, Tevita, Andrew, Dakota, Brandon, Frank, Trayton, Jason, Joel, Marco, Nick, Seth, Joshua, David, Ryan, Craig, Brooklyn, Marlon, John, and Krow. My sisters Laurel, Amanda, Alicia, Maria, Maria, Madison, Brittany, Stephanie, Natalie, Chloe, Emily and Shannon. My mother Julie, my father Richard. My uncles Marc, Mike, Andy, Pat, Brian, Norm, Dan and my aunts Julie, Debbie, Melinda, and Karen. My grandmothers June and Frances, and to my grandfathers William, Gary, and Jerry. My great uncles Jack and Alton, as well as my great aunts Jackie and Jan. My great grandmother Helen, great grandfathers William and Albert, and to the countless other cousins, family members, and friends who truly are my family.

This is the second writing I have done in my free time. My first being "The Mad Hairstyle," which was lost when my father's old computer died. Perhaps one day The Mad Hairstyle will live again.

Books by MUD

The Raven's Nest: Extended Edition

The Raven's Nest 2: A Blonde Man

The Raven's Nest 3: The Hunter's Lair

The Raven Hunter

The Raven Hunter 2: The Mutterfly

The Raven Hunter 3: The Golden Huntress

The Raven World

The Raven World 2: The Raven Master

The Raven World 3: The Butterhorse

The Raven Lord

The Raven Lord 2: Lord Mud

The Raven Lord 3: Rise of the Sphere

INTRODUCTION

A plethora of strange thoughts have gone through my mind during my time in public school and short adult life. Thoughts about life, death, why this and why that, all things that don't really matter. My whole life I have wondered, will I be remembered? It does not impact my positive outlook on life or quality of life, but I always like to think and wonder about my legacy. It's just like how 2Pac asked, "How long will they mourn me?" Maybe if I help people throughout my life they will miss me once I'm gone. Maybe someday children will read this writing and learn from my experiences, and maybe it will help protect them. Maybe they will remember me not by my *real* name, but simply by Mud.

I am 20 years old, and live a life that some would consider to be quite odd. I consider it rather mild in comparison to some of the crazy people in this world, but interesting nonetheless. I went to Placer High School and graduated in 2014, and consider it the best time of my life so far. I stayed fairly quiet throughout high school, never getting in trouble and maintaining a decent GPA. I only kept good grades because it made my mother happy, which in turn made my life better. After graduation, I only stayed in touch with a few of my classmates. Most went off to college and now live a life that looks very boring to me, and some have even started a family already. It will be many years before I am ready for the task of raising a child, but hope to some day have one or two of my own.

What my old classmates do with their lives is not something that interests me greatly. They barely knew my real name by the end of high school. Which is why I'm starting over. They did not know of me as Mud. Mud is a different person, completely changed from the innocent boy I once was. Mud has special meanings to me that you will not understand. You will not understand until you read further into these pages, should you choose to do so. It also spells dum backwards, but only if you're dumb. Don't worry, I'm dumb too.

Mud is the home to many varieties of microscopic life. Such microscopic life has created creatures that have evolved since the Earth's beginning into what they are now in the year 2017 A.D. Creatures that act in mysterious ways and have only been seen by a select few. The few individuals who have encountered these creatures have not always been fortunate enough to escape from them. I was one of the lucky survivors. You will soon discover what these creatures are for yourself. One of these creatures I encountered is to be known as the Raven. She is something beautiful and inexplicable, but absolutely terrifying at her core.

Before I go further into my experience with the Raven creature, let me give you a few more details about my life. I was born in San Diego but moved to a town called Auburn when I was three. Two very different locations that both share the home state of California. Going from a city suburb to tree covered countryside was a vast change of scenery as well as lifestyle for me. My parents would take my sister and me on road trips back to San Diego every year, a journey over 500 miles long.

I loved going for rides in the car, but loved being behind the wheel even more. Daddy would let me sit in his lap and drive on occasion, down our long driveway or in empty parking lots. I even volunteered to mow the lawn just to ride his little green tractor around our yard. Our dogs would run in fear when they saw me on the mower, as I would move the lever from "tortoise" to "hare" and chase after them.

My best friend Christian would come over nearly every day and we would cause all sorts of mayhem. Sword fighting, archery, airsoft. All the dangerous things that my mother hated but we loved to do. We would play video games that were probably inappropriate for our age, feeling the rush from the low resolution violence. Dueling and trading Yu-Gi- Oh! cards, comparing who had the bigger deck.

Life as a child was good in Auburn, and I never wanted elementary school to end. One of the first life lessons I learned was that nothing lasts forever. The wretched disease of age was upon me, and soon enough middle school came along. I hated it. Children transforming into the most annoying, selfish adults on the planet with a growing romantic curiosity. I shut myself away from the teenage drama and lived my life class by class, weekend by weekend.

I felt like my brain was corroding. Puberty was undoing all the years of fun I had in elementary school, like a wave of depression crashing down upon my soul. I had trouble sleeping at night, having nightmares frequently. One in particular put me into the events of the Texas Chainsaw Massacre, where I was never killed but was a witness to all the killings. I had this same nightmare over and over again, and felt like it was some kind of sign. A message from God even.

Suddenly my father's health took a severe turn for the worse, and before I could even say goodbye he was gone. Forever. The wound in my heart was still fresh from the loss of Daddy, but it was about to be cut deeper. My grandfather passed away, and then great grandma Helen shortly after that. I questioned God and why he had done this to me. Was it something I said? Something I did? I was devastated from the loss of my family, and came close to ending my own life. I knew the impact that would have caused on my mother, sister, grandmother, and the rest of my family. Which is why I didn't do it. They meant the world to me, but I never showed it. Something I regret deeply to this day.

Life continued on for the miserable teenaged Mud, and at this point I entered high school. I would like to thank my teachers for being as good at their jobs as they were, because it turned my life around. I grew a stem of creativity and began speaking to other students besides my two best friends Chris and Christian. Woodshop, welding, mechatronics, drafting, art and physics all became passions of mine.

There were so many possibilities in life, so many places to go. How would I get there? I needed a car. With the help of my three favorite women, I passed my written and physical driving exams at the DMV. I saw an ad for a 1983 Chevy Blazer for sale, and mother said I could have it. It was yellow with old school red flames, like something out of a Steve McQueen movie. She was slow and hefty, but was my pride and joy that I loved. I felt so free and independent. My life ambitions as a teenage driver, as a wild boy at the core. My core. It would change me forever.

My whole life had come up to this moment and there I was still breathing. I never got that "good ass whipping" that was apparently required as a child. Perhaps my father was supposed to deliver it to me but never got around to it before he passed away. I lived free and wild and yet somehow, because of my dearest mother, stayed alive through it all. Call your mother before you read any further. Do it for me, Mud, who you do not know but I would like to know you. Tell me what is so interesting in your life, how you spend your alone time, much like this time. Call your mother if you can, but know if you cannot that it is still alright. We do not live forever and whatever time we still have should only be spent being productive with ourselves or with family.

Years have gone by since I graduated high school, and so many things have happened in that time. I did not go to college, but learned more than any school could ever teach me. My sister choose to become a nurse, and just recently completed her many years of schooling. I would like to congratulate her on her success and wish her a good future wherever she may choose to go.

I chose a different career path. Something more dirty. Something more dangerous. Something that will always stay with me no matter what. I do not know where I will end up.

CHAPTER 1

The first time I saw her was exactly 8 months ago when brother Brandon showed me to her on the television screen. She was in a VHS, a diabolical, emotionally distraught creature in need of love. She would evolve right before your eyes, turning from an angel into a winged demon. Months would go by before I was to see her again, except the next time would be in real life. Her Spirit must have been following me since the day I first saw her on the VHS tape, for a series of unexplained events were to occur regularly for the next 8 months.

I was never alone when these events occurred. It was always with some of my brothers or sisters. The first occurrence happened with brother Tenny in Balboa Park. We had ventured into the Imax theater in the afternoon on a very beautiful sunny day. The feature presentation was a National Geographic film called "Extreme Weather." Upon finishing the movie and exiting the theater, it was completely dark with heavy downpours. It was like we had walked right into the movie. At first, we embraced this rain as a change to the regular Southern California sun and normal drought that we live in. We must have looked completely insane frolicking in the rain, excited to have some new weather. However, our frolicking may have led us to a place we were not supposed to go.

Our path led to a small overlook where a book lay open face down. The book was hardly even wet from the rain, as if someone had just recently pulled it out from their purse or backpack and began to read it.

Except there was no reader in sight. We looked around, and no one was around. We then peeked over the edge of the short wall that the book lay on top of. Way down below, perhaps a hundred foot drop, was a bush that appeared to have been landed on, but there was no body or evidence besides the smashed bush. Had the book caused its reader to attempt suicide? Curiosity overcame Tenny and me, and he decided he would keep the book for himself. This book was titled "Burton."

Brother Brandon called shortly after and said that he was around Balboa park with Marcus. I told them to come to our location immediately. Within minutes they arrived, curious as to what Tenny and I were so concerned about. Tenny showed them the book, and pointed to the bush. "Let's go down there," said Brandon. Down we went, all the while being soaked with rain.

The path to the bottom was paved and about wide enough for a golf cart to travel on. It wound down the hill and went underneath a bridge before heading back towards where the smashed bush was. We reached the bush and there was absolutely nothing. No blood, no personal belongings, just a bush that appeared to be crushed under the weight of a 200 pound person.

I did not hear about any missing or suicidal people on the news that could have been our bush man. Maybe it was Burton himself, leaping out from the pages of his book trying to end it all. A sad character Burton must have been, unable to keep himself together. May he find peace wherever he has gone.

The next occurrence was on a weekend trip with my brothers Tenny, Brandon, and Frank. We had planned to go hiking in the trails of Palomar mountain and get some nice mountain air. What we did not plan for was the huge amount of fresh snowfall and freezing temperatures. We were in Tenny's supercharged red Mustang, possibly the worst American-made vehicle for offroading.

We had set out early in the morning so that it would be around lunchtime once we arrived. We had plenty of food and drinks packed in our small disposable ice chest. All of us were having a great time, with the windows down and country music blasting. We sped through Pala where Tenny pointed out one of his favorite places to go dirt bike riding. The road narrowed as it came closer to the mountain edge, and soon became shoulderless. Signs for falling rocks were scattered along the side of the road, and sure enough our path ahead was blocked by small boulders.

We had come too far to be stopped now, so Tenny pulled the Mustang over and we all jumped out. As we began clearing the boulders out of the road, a car full of older women approached and stopped. They offered to help but weren't able to do so because of the weight of the rocks, which were easily over 50 pounds. We finished clearing the road and proceeded on our way up Palomar Mountain.

As we drove up the mountain the temperature began to drop, and the trees started to have a thin layer of frost on their leaves. Soon both sides of the road were completely covered in snow. Tenny was confident he could maneuver the Mustang across the black ice, but I had my doubts when we began to drift around every corner. He finally gave in and said it was time to turn back. However, he did not want to return the way we just came. We turned at the only intersection in the small town atop the mountain.

Children were playing in the snow along the side of the road, with their parents keeping a close eye on them. I reminisced about playing in the snow at Lake Tahoe as a child, and almost wanted to jump out and play with them. My brothers did not share the same feeling as I, probably because we were all in Tee shirts and shorts. We stopped at a scenic overlook to use the restroom, and I walked to the edge to take in the view. It was breath taking. From the overlook I could see a lake way off in the distance. This was to be our destination.

The lake was called Lake Henshaw, a small body of water surrounded by grasslands and also the home to a biker resort. We parked the Mustang on the side of the road about a quarter mile away from the water and far from the resort. From the car we could see a man fishing in the lake with a dog playing in the water. The shore of the lake was protected by a short electric fence, but I'm not really sure what it was they were trying to keep in or out. It would take much more than a measly little electric fence to stop the four of us, and we went right over it. I even grabbed the fence on purpose and enjoyed the slight tickle it gave me.

Tenny led the way through the tall grass, which was full of insects and completely soaked our shoes in ankle deep mud. Pterodactyl-sized birds flew overhead and looked so majestic, like feathered aircraft. As we walked closer to the water, we all saw it: The Rock. A large, rainbow moss-covered boulder that looked like something from another planet. Naturally, the four of us walked over to The Rock to get a closer examination. It was magnificent. Tenny placed his hand on it and the most unbelievable thing happened. It moved. Yes, The Rock moved. It did not get up and walk away or slide across the rocky soil surrounding it. No, it changed shape, morphing around Tenny's fingers, leaving indents where he pressed that then popped back up when he released. It was not the moss that was morphing, it was The Rock itself.

The weather seemed to change as Tenny pressed the Rock. When we had ventured out from the car and crossed the electric fence, the sky was clear and sunny. Clouds began to rapidly move in as The Rock transformed, and soon it was a heavenly mist. A massive rainbow formed across the sky, the most perfect rainbow I have ever seen. All of us were witnesses to it, and all of us were mind blown.

The rainbow disappeared and the clouds began to darken. A torrential downpour of warm rain fell from the sky, leaving us soaked. We quickly left The Rock and began to walk back towards the car. However, the lake appeared to be rising as the rain came pouring down. Soon we were *in* the lake, up to our ankles in the murky water. We picked up our pace and jumped over the electric fence. By the time we were back at the car, the clouds were gone and the sun was out once more.

I looked back at the lake, and the man with his dog were still there. It was as if nothing had ever happened. This was approximately February, some 4 months ago, and I can picture it perfectly to this day.

I do not know if the Spirit of the Raven from the VHS or the Spirit of Burton had an effect on The Rock, but I have not been able to relocate The Rock since that day. Perhaps The Rock possessed some kind of spirit of its own and moved to a new location. Maybe it was the mother of all rocks, thanking us for moving her children out of the road earlier that day. Neither my brothers nor I could believe what we had seen, but it was all too real.

The next and final unnatural encounter before meeting the Raven occurred in Guajome Regional Park. My brothers Tenny, Brandon, Marcus and myself were there to explore the park after driving by it so many times in the past. It is a beautiful place, with several trails that go through a wonderfully preserved natural habitat and home to a very family friendly campground. This was a sunny Saturday in May, not too long ago.

The trail we choose ran along the side of the campground and through tall grass adjacent to Guajome Lake. The trail crossed over an old wooden bridge with a pond full of tadpoles below it. Past the bridge the trail ran underneath the 76, and the acoustics there were incredible. My JBL portable speaker sounded like concert speakers under the highway, and the cars passing overhead created an awesome sound effect.

We continued down the paved path towards a small dirt parking lot which was the head to an off-road trail. Foolishly, we decided to wander down this rugged path. Walking down the trail we could hear voices behind the bushes, and an eerie feeling was felt by all of us. Unoccupied tents and makeshift sleeping areas were scattered all over the sides of the trail.

Suddenly, an old homeless man came yelling and chasing his girlfriend out of the bushes, but once he saw us he stopped shouting and slowed his pace down. After deciding she was alright, we decided it was best to return to the parking lot and back towards the park. They followed us back to the parking lot with about 50 feet of dispersion from us. The couple then climbed into their red Chevy S10.

Brandon had recognized the homeless couple, but could not remember exactly from where. When he saw them get in the truck, he knew immediately. He had seen this very same couple earlier in the day at Albertsons, where they had previously climbed into the truck with a bottle of Jack Daniels in a paper bag. I can only assume that alcohol is the cause of their misfortune, and for that I have no remorse for them.

The homeless encounter in Guajome was eye opening to me, because I had never seen poverty to that level in person since I lived back in Auburn. The railroad tracks of Auburn are home to perhaps hundreds of homeless who make a living by recycling glass and metal and begging on busy street corners. I do not have much pity for them, because they have only failed themselves. All they need to do is visit the library and educate themselves to get back into regular society. If you are homeless and reading this, I congratulate you for heading back in the right direction towards success. I have already made an outline for my entire life, with backup plans in case things don't turn out exactly according to plan. I plan to live off the road and the Earth someday, just as our ancestors once did.

Now back to the trail in Guajome Park. On our way back we cut through the campground and discovered an incredible children's playground. Brandon saw the abstract jungle gym and swing sets from afar, and said we had to go check it out. The entire area was shaded under a large painted metal gazebo that reminded me of an old sailboat. The ground was compacted rubber and gave great springiness to your step, allowing one to leap distances with ease. A strange diamond structure that looked like something out of The Matrix was in the corner of the gazebo. It changed shapes from different perspectives, and was like something a spider would make out of its web.

Brandon decided in his usual fashion that he had to climb to the top of this structure and claim the playground as his own fun land. I decided to take a picture.

After enjoying the view from the top of the diamond, Brandon and I then decided to go on the swings. Tenny and Marcus hated how childish we were acting, but Brandon and I were having a blast. Another man was already on the swings, minding his own business with headphones in. He was about our age, but very pale white with blonde hair. He looked like he had not been outside in weeks.

Brandon said "Hello" to him. He told us, "Just taking a break to stretch my legs from all these video games!" I could tell. Yes, as a former gamer myself, spending far too much of my childhood indoors on the PlayStation and my custom built PC. Admittedly I still enjoy opening my Steam library and randomly selecting from my collection of games. We asked what his name was, and he told us "John." One of my two best friends in Auburn had a brother named John who was very similar to this John on the swings.

Brandon asked what games he played, and he said mainly "Star Wars The Old Republic." A very fun game, I thought to myself. Brandon asked if he played any modern games, but John was strictly old school. We had a good chat about games and gaming systems new and old, and it was good to see someone who was very well informed on the subject. We said goodbye to John and he said goodbye as well. Brandon, Marcus, Tenny and myself then walked to a picnic bench under a tree about 50 feet away.

There was a beautiful wedding in the distance, and I thought how that's probably going to be my sister soon. We looked back at the swing sets where we had just come from, but something wasn't right. John was gone, and the swings were completely still. The parking lot was approximately 50 feet in the opposite direction, and he was not there. John had vanished. ＊ It seemed as though, unless John silently sprinted away from us the very second we left, he must have never been there at all. Yet, all four of us saw him. Brandon and I talked to him. But he was gone. Never to be seen again. We pondered the mysterious John on our drive home in Tenny's Mustang, but could not ponder too hard because Tenny was blasting 2Pac the whole way back. This was the night of May 20th.

The evening of May 26 I had plans to go to San Juan Capistrano, north of San Clemente, with brother Tenny. We had essentially planned to plan for nothing. This was our first mistake, as we are usually smart enough to predict our wild adventures instead of just letting it all happen by surprise. Tenny and I were two completely separate individuals brought together by a love of music, and living life to the fullest. No bad intentions were ever had by us, just positive vibes and controlled chaos.

We live in this new society of mindless drones, where Tenny and I do not belong. These drones are like little creatures, plagued with thousands of years of mistakes and arguments similar to those that would occur later on this night. Two brothers driving to go meet with this friend, of the female variety. The internet is home to many meet and greet sites that are designed to create new friendships or kindle a relationship. The issue being that the drones on these websites are not always the same online as they are in person. The Raven came to me on one of these sites where we were considered "a match." How deceptive she was.

She was a mysterious thing. History and evolution have combined in a strange way to create this loving being. She was something out of an art museum mixed with the mind of an alien from the future. Her profile seemed too good to be true, but even if she was remotely close to what she claimed I would be happy. We messaged and got along excellently, arranging for this meetup on the 26th. I was so excited to be meeting up with the apparent girl of my dreams.

So I thought. Lots of thoughts were had by me throughout my life, much like the ones you are thinking right now. Which brings me to another point. What are you thinking? What is your image of all the events that have taken place up until now? Do you think I'm crazy? I assure you I am not. Are these two brothers out to kill something or someone tonight? Possibly, but not this girl. My hope was to discover an awesome new friend, a friend from this place called the internet. She had a difficult name to remember, so Tenny and I simply referred to her as Raven. Little was known about this friend to meet.

If you have friends you do not treat like family, they are not your friends. They are just peasants in your life. Peasants are like pests. Pests, flying around on the internet stinging where they please. It is only when they step out of their door and into the real world when they realize how big a pest they are. But some are so pestuous that they do not even monitor this aspect of themselves. Pause once more from reading further. The password is claw. How are you as a person? Are you a pest?

Consider what you say to others over the internet as if they were right in front of you. Because what happens on the internet does not stay on the internet, it is projected into the eyes of a real person who may then interpret something into something it Is not. Is someone around you right now, sitting at another table or walking in your direction? Look at them. Are they a pest? I am not even looking at them but I can already tell you they are a pest. I know they are. It is simply what humans are. Pests. To this earth. The lock is tiger. And just like this pest we were driving to meet, pests have needs. The particular pest I was about to infest my evening with had needs which could only be provided by a laboratory. Laboratories that study pests, and how their brains work and malfunction.

The mythical land of the internet where I discovered this pest is a strange place. I wish it didn't exist but am so amazed at what it is and what it does. It's just a thing that kids are born into now that has this massive life-changing tool for free. A tool that can be used for free at your local library, which I truly hope you are currently reading this in. Libraries are the devolved internet. Where the true humans of this earth grew up, studying the records of our ancestors and building off their knowledge base. Being called weird and judged from head to toe, it's all natural.

Insults are not something one should worry about receiving, nor be afraid to dish out. They are just words, but know that words can have their consequences. Reputations are created, possibly a reputation you do not want to have, as is the case with me. It's times like these where you just have to look back at yourself and say "Fuck!" I'm alive. I apologize for my language. It won't happen again for the rest of this read I promise. You remember my name right? Ok, I thought so.

I love all people, but can't live with any of them. So I find myself in the hills, alone and unafraid. My name will be Mud from now on. It is not a first name, it is not a last name. Just Mud. Three letters. Very easy to spell, and conveniently rhymes with a lot of things. I'm not putting copywrites on this name or any legal entitlements. This life is far too short to waste time in those affairs, so I choose the happy and productive route. Speaking of productivity, I congratulate the earth for spawning the Raven pest I was discussing earlier. My train of thought tends to interrupt itself, but bear with me. You have made it this far.

She is a thing of angels to be glorified. But only at first glance. She projects herself in ways even I am too tame to project into society, and she does it with manners and pride. I love her in that respect. But I wish I could love her for more. For beyond first glance, she is a powerful pest. A queen pest. The queen pest of society was to be met by me on this evening.

I asked Tenny if he would join me for the ride, because I was quite nervous about meeting Raven. Later in the night he divorced me from the family because of the sting that the queen pest would inflict on me. But that is getting too far ahead of the story. I apologize, it is getting very late for me. It is 5 in the morning and I still haven't slept, so I must go rest now. Perhaps you should too. Sleep is a critical part of the pest life cycle, but use your time how you want. This is America after all.

MUD

Consider this the beginning of Chapter 2 of this read with only 1 chapter. Because things may change once I wake up. And a lot of things go thru my head while I sleep. Like right now. Do you hear that? Probably not. But it's Logic saying like whoa and it's got me like whoa. Wow.

Welcome back. I hope you are well rested from last night's events. I cannot say that I am. It is of no matter. My genes and life experiences always surprise me with something new on a daily basis. I have never gone to college yet I feel that all of yesterday's happenings converted me into a doctor, a nurse, a warrior, and taxi driver simultaneously. Just hours before setting out on the highway with my brother, I was going on a nature hike, out away from all civilization.

The air out there does wonders for a person. Living under the sun as our ancestors once did for even just 24 hours can completely change your outlook on life. Perhaps once you get some more rest and do some proper preparation, you can head out to mother nature and see what I mean. The little critters wandering around, the birds chirping, the flowers doing whatever it is they do. It is amazing. Let me progress further into our night with the Raven pest.

My brother, a heavy set, wild southern boy with an unpredictable behavior, had very few limits on anything in life. I know that someday he will ride his dirt bike straight into his grave. That's only if he makes it long enough to survive the crazy adventures with me. He hates me for always being who I really am, which is truly just a regular person. I was never one to lie in my favor or double cross people in ordinary conversation. Tenny would lie straight to your face in regular conversation if he did not like you. I always hated that.

I used to decipher the truth out of him when he could never just speak the truth to begin with. It made communicating a nightmare but spontaneous adventures like this night with the Raven a blast. I loved him for that. Few people in this cruel world have my back as I would have theirs. How many people could you call right now if you really needed to kill someone with out the rest of the pests finding out? They are contacts that should never be used, but are always there for you. I have many such contacts like these, and it would require more than two hands to count them all. Well, Tenny and I of course had no intentions of killing this girl or anyone else tonight, but naturally my brother and I are always on guard.

We drove the 48 miles from my residence to the Ravens nest with positive vibes and not a single worry in mind. The road was lively with Memorial Day weekend drivers and California's finest men and women in uniform. Driving laws are perhaps the only laws I can take seriously, because I simply do not have time to deal with getting in an accident. Far too many legalities and formal matters involved in car crashes. This country's justice system and judgment system is just wrong if you ask me, which is why I avoid it altogether. I am truly not even concerned about minor injuries that may occur in accidents. Things that might prevent me from walking away are all that concern me. As they should to you as well. Look out for your life on the road and I will look out for mine, and we can all drive in harmony. Thank you. Now, my brother and I both like to stay hydrated at all times and consequently require frequent restroom stops or a bush to do business in, depending on the time and location.

The nicest Shell gas station I have ever encountered in my entire life was exactly 1.6 miles away from the nest of the queen pest. Tenny and I both released a flood upon the restroom urinals before browsing the store aisles for random treasures. I gazed upon the lottery machine in the corner and tried to buy a $5 scratcher, but the old rusty thing refused to take my money. It must not have been worth it.

We left the shop and saw a group of teenagers in the parking lot sitting in their car. This normally would not have caught my attention, except one of them was holding a freshly caught salmon in his lap that was still flopping and very alive. I do not care to wonder what they had in store for that poor fish, but I was rather curious where they got it from. We left the gas station and continued down the 74. Closer to the Raven's nest we came. I began to feel my heart pumping as fast as my tires were spinning. Was this beautiful internet pest really going to be the Angel of my dreams? We were so soon to find out.

My cell phone navigation almost failed to give me proper warning of the sharp right turn to pull into the Raven's neighborhood. Tires were squealing and I could feel the agony of my 1997 Jeep. Yes, my dream car that shared the same age as I, manufactured in 1996. This car is my only child and I will keep it forever. Vehicles are like friends, if you don't cherish them now you will die without them. This is how I feel about all the luxury things I purchase. They all have a purpose, and without them I could not live my life in complete happiness.

You might be wondering what happened to my first mechanical child, the '83 Blazer. Well, one day I was making the drive from Auburn to Grass Valley along Highway 49 when she nearly killed me. Her engine shut off as I was flying down a steep hill, causing me to lose power steering and power brakes. I wrestled the steering wheel and stood on the brake pedal, eventually coming to a stop as the road began to travel back uphill. She was never the same after that. Spontaneously dying and having all sorts of problems, so I sold her. It was not a decision I took lightly, but I was not ready to die in a car crash just yet. You might just see her with her new owner if you pass through Auburn. She is legendary, but just not meant to be with me.

After the Blazer came my 2nd pride and joy, a 2001 Chevy S10. This was the newest four wheeled vehicle I have ever purchased to date, but it was very low tech which is why I loved it. Manual windows, manual door locks, nothing fancy. She could take a mean beating. The previous owner had lowered her slightly, but I drove it like a lifted 4x4. She glided over mud holes and sand pits like a hovercraft, and never once got stuck. She could drift around wet parking lots with ease, between the pathetic traction of the tires and complete lack of weight in the rear. I loved it.

The same time I had the 510 I also bought a 1994 Geo Metro. It cost me $250, and was the best deal of my life. I cannot recommend this car any higher, everyone should buy one or two. 5he drank equal parts oil and gasoline, but could survive a nuclear war. Parents, this is an excellent 1st car for your son or daughter. Kids, don't judge a book by its cover, that is the most fun you will have from a car. However, the Jeep was my dream car, and I had to sell the 510 and the Geo in order to purchase it. It was definitely worth it. Now then, let's get back to the Jeep with Tenny and myself.

We made the second right hand turn into the neighborhood and I could at last see the nest. It was two stories with a large garage and slim windows on the second floor, which were ideal for a lookout. I did not see any cameras around the outside of the nest, but had a strong feeling that I was being watched. It was so creepy.

I pulled out my phone and sent the Raven a message that we were finally outside. 5he had no idea that I was bringing Tenny along, and I still wonder how different the next few hours would have gone had I left my brother at home. Minutes went by before she sent me an "OK." I was so nerve wracked. I had spent my life plagued with a social anxiety that resulted in me having very few friends and even fewer significant others throughout public school. My mother always awaited the day I would bring home a girlfriend for her to meet, but I never delivered it to her.

At last I saw the door open. There she was. The Raven. In the flesh. I was taken aback somewhat by her height, perhaps around 5 feet. It was of no matter to me. Her body proportions matched so beautifully that I thought I was in love. Her hair was unique with small dread braids mixed into an oriental bun. It was blonde with dark roots, and shined in the sun. I was speechless.

She came out of her nest talking on her cellphone, which irritated me slightly as a first impression. I am cultured more towards face to face conversation, and considered it rather rude and immature on her behalf. I could let it slide this time.

She opened the door and got in the Jeep, and gave a friendly "Hello." I was so excited. A nice, pretty girl that actually seemed like a decent member of today's society. She described herself as a special needs student teacher. It would be hours later before I realized what that actually meant. The Raven then noticed Tenny in the back seat who also gave a friendly "Hello." She was surprised to see him, as I had given her no warning of his accompaniment to our evening. We left the nest with little small talk and rather awkward shyness among the three of us.

Earlier that day Tenny had driven his Mustang along the 74 and was eager to show us the canyon that the highway ran through. It did not occur to me that the Raven had probably already seen this canyon dozens of times since she lived so close by, but I trusted my brother. So we took a right turn out of the neighborhood and made our way towards the national forest lands.

As we approached the canyon, an SUV driving the opposite direction flashed his lights at me. * I was rather confused by this as it was still broad day light so headlights were not needed. There weren't any cops waiting to ambush me either, because I could see miles down the road and it was open fields on both sides. I flipped my headlights on anyways just to please Tenny.

We proceeded down the long straight road and approached a sharp blind turn. Around the corner, traffic was completely halted and caught me by surprise. We stopped and figured it was just a slight delay, but no. At least 5 minutes went by, then emergency vehicles with their lights on came flying from behind us heading towards our destination. Whatever happened must have just occurred moments before we arrived. I decided it was time to take a different route, and turned the Jeep around. Tenny and the Raven both seemed interested in waiting, but I had lost my patience. With more continuous awkward silence, we proceeded back the way we came, past the Raven's neighborhood and onto the 5.

Before Tenny and I picked up the Raven, I had planned out different topics and discussion ideas. However, it was all failing and I had nothing to talk about. We drove with the radio doing all the talking, and I felt like the night was already a disaster. Tenny turned out to be making things much worse than I anticipated.

We continued down the 5 until San Onofre beach, where Tenny begged for me to pull over to go pee. I reluctantly agreed, only because of the look of desperation on his face. During my alone time with the Raven, I asked when her birthday was. She said "September." I was pleasantly surprised to share the same birth month as her. I asked what year. She replied "1996." This came as much more of a surprise to me, and I knew she was lying. Her internet profile said she was a year younger than me. Was she just messing with me? Did I already tell her my exact birthday? Had she done research on me before we picked her up? I did not care to ask her what day and continue the taunt.

Tenny at last returned from his extra long whiz break. Little did I know that we were on a one way road to the beach, so after Tenny climbed back into the Jeep we had to continue the wrong direction until I could turn around. At last we got back on the 5 and took the Harbor Drive exit to Oceanside. The Raven saw the In-N-Out up ahead and asked if we could stop. Tenny and I being hungry ourselves, I decided why not.

Tenny noticed something odd in the parking lot, it was a vehicle that we had seen much earlier in the day. A large blue Sprinter van with several large antennas sticking out of the roof, and heavily tinted windows. The last time we had seen it was right after leaving our residence. The van had Tenny freaking out a little but I told him to relax, it was just a coincidence. Little did I know that Tenny was actually onto something.

We gave our orders and I paid for everyone. Tenny did not order anything but ended up eating most of the food. Food is not something I consider a necessity in life, just a luxury. Continuous hydration and fresh air is all that keeps me alive, with an occasional source of protein. I pay close attention to my diet, thanks to my nurse mother and sister. I do not see the reasoning of body builders and gym dwellers, because it has no practical application. Free running, shadow boxing, and self discipline is the best workout for a human being, and it is completely free. I can out run and dodge a slow clumsy body builder before they could do any real damage to me, plus I'm armed almost everywhere I go. Some of you are probably questioning this right about now, but I promise you I'm not making this up.

We continued down the 76 towards our residence, known to us as The Studio. Shower Thoughts Studios is what I call it, because all of my most ambitious ideas seem to occur in the shower there. Music, movie ideas, and book ideas much like this one have all occurred in that tiny aging shower. I have big plans that no one else knows about, and I have no plans to share them. The Studio is my little side project, my hidden treasure. The Raven would be the first stranger to see it in person.

After eating a small portion of her burger, the Raven finally began talking with complete sentences and holding a conversation. She talked about spending most of her life in Orange County and how she rarely visited this area. She also talked about how she didn't have a car, which I thought was very strange for a girl her age. My whole life rotated around my various vehicles, and I couldn't imagine what I would do without them. Walk? Nonsense.

She mentioned how her dream car was a Jeep much like my own, and I praised her for her taste in cars. Tenny asked if he could play music until we got back to the Studio and I accepted his offer. He put on some old Gorillaz followed by electronic dance music. The Raven did not seem particularly interested.

At last we made it. I pulled into the Studio's parking lot and got out of the car. My back and legs crackled from sitting for so long. The Raven and Tenny clearly heard the pops. I hate long drives. I try to get a massage once a month if my bank account allows for it, but that is not always the case. Life takes quite a toll on the human body, and people neglect themselves far too often.

We went inside and Tenny offered Raven a Mike's Harder Lemonade from the fridge, which she gladly accepted. I was eager to show her some of the recordings that Brandon, Marcus, and myself had recorded. It is the work of Lost Minds and Mud, and will someday in the future be released for all to listen to. For now it is kept on two redundant hard drives inside The Studio.

It was not too long ago when Brandon and Marcus formed what they call "Lost Minds." They come from two different backgrounds but both love to rap, and are very good at it. When they record they stand right next to each other in the booth, taking turns on the mic and hyping each other up. We listened to about 5 songs worth of recording before I paused the music. I was dying to get some input and criticism from the Raven.

She gave compliments but I feel like she was just saying what I wanted to hear. All the audio was completely raw, and while I admit is not bad, it's not the greatest, yet. A side note: look out for Mud and Lost Minds in the future, we are coming. I directed her away from the recording area of the Studio and back towards the living area.

We moved to the couch. A cheap, poorly made brown thing that probably belongs in a dumpster. However, the couch is not the focal point of the room. It is the television and the accompanying sound system. 50 inch 4k televisions are truly something magnificent that we have in this day and age. We watched some of my favorite music videos by A$AP, Kendrick Lamar, Schoolboy Q, Gorillaz, and Green Day.

Green Day was one of my favorite bands growing up, particularly the song "Wake Me Up When September Ends," because of my birthday. I had somehow never seen the music video as a child, so I decided to click on it. The video is considerably longer than the actual song, but I was pleasantly surprised. Check it out if you've never seen it. I then asked the Raven to show us a music video from one of her favorite bands.

She pulled up a punk music video with very graphic footage about "F*** the Police." No, I'm not referring to NWA. Trust me, this is so horrible that I do not wish to give you the band name and give them unnecessary popularity or views. It was truly disturbing. After watching the police brutality, Tenny put on some country to help our hearts and minds recover but the Raven was not interested. She called a "friend" who apparently was having some emotional crisis. ★ I was getting uncomfortable and asked if we could all go for a walk outside. Tenny and the Raven agreed.

Before going on our walk, Tenny wanted to stop and smoke. We walked to the corner outside of the Studio, near the street. Tenny attempted to start a conversation while he smoked, but the Raven did not seem to understand what he was saying. I felt weird having to continuously clarify what he was saying to her, and just wanted to get going. He finished his cigarette, and we began our journey down the dark streets.

Allow me to pause for a moment, I have left out one important detail. The Raven had worn these ridiculous high heel boot-looking shoes that looked truly awful for walking in, so I offered her my camouflage Crocs instead. So the Raven was at this point now in a nice jacket, nice shirt, nice pants, and camouflage Crocs. You can refer to the cover of this book if you would like to see her original shoes for yourself. Now then, back to our journey.

We walked down the street and to the bottom of the hill that the Studio was built atop of. It was very dark down there, and a man was in a driveway charging his truck battery with some jumper cables. I have charged plenty of batteries and jumped plenty of cars in my lifetime, but this man's setup looked very unsafe. Bare wires were exposed and connected with what appeared to be a homemade extension cord. You could hear the sound of the electricity and see sparks flaring from the wires. We briskly continued down the road into a regular neighborhood, where I noticed a garage door was open.

Walking past the garage, we could see an old couple inside watching a movie on their dusty aging recliners. The flat screen television was mounted on the wall above a small workbench, with all the cables hidden away. I liked this setup. We waved hello and continued walking down the street. Tenny had to pee yet again, and ran off to a bush in a dark corner. I slowly kept walking with the Raven as to not appear to be loitering outside someone's home in the middle of the night. A car drove past but I do not think they saw Tenny peeing or suspected anything unusual.

Our walk through the neighborhood began to ascend to the top of the hill that faced towards The Studio. The Raven apparently did not have much stamina, as she was breathing very heavily once we reached the top. Tenny stopped to smoke again, which visibly disgusted the exhausted Raven. The night air was cool and humid, and the slight breeze was very refreshing. The sky was clear and I could see the lights of Fallbrook and Oceanside off in the distance.

Tenny began discussing politics, something I do not like to talk about frequently. I am not Republican or Democrat, just somewhere in the middle with mixed views. Freedom is my political party. A large black Cadillac SUV passed by and we made a joke about Donald Trump jumping out to shake our hands. The Raven seemed shocked that we could even say such a thing, she was clearly a Democrat.

Moments later, the Raven began to twitch. She started speaking without any logic, causing Tenny to give me a look of confusion. I suggested we start walking back to the Studio, and Tenny agreed. The Raven exclaimed "OoKkEeE!!" More confusion between myself and Tenny. We began heading back down the hill and at this point the Raven seemed very alarmed and jittery.

She drifted off the sidewalk and into the street, and nearly collided with a parked car. I pulled her back and guided her along the sidewalk, but she was like a wild dog off her leash. I was trying my best to prevent her from stumbling over the cracks and bumps on the side walk but didn't want to make a scene. A car passed by and I can only imagine what they were thinking. We looked like some crazy siblings out for a midnight walk. After reaching the bottom of the hill and beginning our final ascent towards the Studio, the Raven began to severely spaz and twitch, even scream.

Tenny did not take her seriously and demanded she shut up, but I knew something was wrong. Tenny and I each wrapped an arm around her to assist up the hill, but it was no use. She collapsed, screaming on the way to the ground. She landed directly on her back, which looked very painful. Tenny yelled at her to get up immediately, and she gave a creepy laugh but got up. She stumbled ahead of us towards the Studio, then Tenny grabbed me by the shoulder. "She said she was a special education *teacher*, right?" I nodded. "I think she's actually a student!"

At this point I was so confused with the situation at hand that I didn't know what to do anymore. My instincts were telling me that the Raven needed medical assistance, but Tenny was confident that she was just making a scene. We made it back to the studio and I sat her on the couch and rushed to get her some water. After I fetched a full glass, she took a sip then screamed yet again and violently twitched, spilling the entire cup over the couch. This was both amusing and irritating, but luckily it was just water. However, she would not stop screaming. Tenny advised her to quiet down, when she suddenly turned and bit his arm.

People have a strange tendency to fight one another. Whether it's physically hurting each other or verbally abusing one another, humans just like to fight. I do not share this feeling, because if I truly have a problem with someone they will certainly know. I am not one to get angry easily, but Tenny and the Raven were pushing me over the edge. One should always arm themselves with whatever is around them, because it is mind power over muscle power. The brain is a magical thing that I cannot comprehend, and the brain of the Raven is something truly remarkable.

Tenny was on the brink of swinging at her, however he held back. I grabbed my keys and said we were leaving, but Tenny said we did not need to, that we could get the Raven under control. I actually care about my neighbors and just wanted to give them the courtesy of silence at 1 in the morning, plus I couldn't tell if the Raven was about to die on my couch. What a mess that would have been.

Tenny became angry when I kept insisting that we leave. I decided enough was enough. I grabbed the Raven by her hand and guided her to the Jeep. Tenny followed me outside, shouting and cursing for me to come back. I'm not sure if it was just instinct or my brain trying to get payback at Tenny, but I locked the door to the Studio on the way out. His car keys were still inside. I jumped in my car and left him on the street, where he was still shouting.

The Raven was screaming and violently twitching in the Jeep, but luckily didn't break anything on my iron horse. If there's one thing that gets me angry, it's when people break my stuff. I tried to calm her down and talk to her but it was no use, I received only strange noises and crying in response. I proceeded to drive in silence, not talking to her and not playing any music. That is something I never do.

The Raven gradually went into silent mode and I thought she may have gone brain dead, but she was clearly still alive. She curled up into somewhat of a fetal position, or as close as one could get to it with a seatbelt on. After a few miles of driving and silently talking to myself, I decided it was best that I take her back to her home. Perhaps her parents or caregivers would know what to do or had the necessary medication.

The silence was very relaxing and allowed me to concentrate, and also let me hear the maintenance that the Jeep is going to need in the near future. Then two loud noises simultaneously went off, my fuel warning light and my cellphone ringing with a call from Tenny. By some miracle the Raven did not wake up, and I silenced my phone. Tenny could wait in my mind.

I continued driving the 76 towards the 5, but knew I would have to fuel up at some point. I searched for the least inhabited gas station in case the Raven started screaming again and someone called the authorities. I found an independent station with only one car at the pumps and decided this was it. I slowly pulled in and shut off the Jeep. The Raven remained asleep.

I tried to use my debit card but was told I had insufficient funds to my surprise. Frantically I fumbled through my wallet, pulling out my credit card which worked fortunately. Unfortunately, this pump must have been the slowest pump in the county and it took an eternity to fill the Jeep's tank. I pulled out my phone and texted Tenny that everything was alright but he did not respond. He was obviously very upset still, granted he had good reason. It was no matter, the Raven was still curled up asleep, and I continued on to the highway. I felt my phone vibrate once more as Tenny tried to call again but I did not want to answer and break the silence of the car ride.

Meanwhile at the Studio, Tenny gave up on calling me. The Mustang was unlocked so he changed into his gym clothes which were lying in the back seat. He popped his headphones in, and headed towards downtown Fallbrook. Now, Fallbrook is a very family friendly place with a positive, small town feel. In the daytime I doubt there is a much safer place in southern California, but at night everything changes. There are few street lights, with an abundance of shadows and dark corners for creatures and pests to hide in. Night walks used to be one of my favorite forms of stress relief, but I have seen things around these parts that have made me too afraid.

The first time my suspicions began to be raised about the safety of nighttime Fallbrook was when I was walking with a friend around 10 o'clock one night. We ascended the hill over Mission Road where a small road lies hidden, and the shoulders of the road become very narrow. There were no cars around, but we could hear voices approximately 50 feet away. Their speaking was completely unintelligible and the odor of crack pipes was strong. It frightened the both of us, so we quickly turned around and returned the way we came.

The final straw for me was a separate night when I was out for a walk alone. It was a cool night in January and I was walking the same route I had taken with my friend before, the one with the crack heads. I was coming down the hill towards the cafe when I saw movement behind a building across the street. I crept closer, sticking to the shadows. It was too late for me to turn back at this point. As I got within earshot, it appeared like a group of people were dancing in a circle. I watched for a couple minutes, and believe what I saw was a ring of Satan worshippers performing some kind of ceremony. They were chanting something as they twirled around, but I could not make it out. I wanted to record their acts but was terrified of what would happen if they saw me. So I slowly crept down the street and back towards the safety of the Studio.

As Tenny continued his jog towards Main Avenue, the streets began to get darker. It was a Friday night, but nobody was around. Tenny has never been one to be afraid of the dark or afraid to be alone, but he had a strange feeling in his gut. He turned the corner from Alvarado to Main and headed up the street.

All the shops were of course closed at this hour, but Tenny saw something moving in a window. This is how he later described it to me, and swore on his grandmother's grave that this is what he saw. "You know the old Mortal Kombat games...?" I replied, "Of course." He told me, "Picture the reptile creature from that." I could imagine It, like a slithering alligator with a face in the shop window. "It was moving, and it just kept looking at me." Had I not experienced the Satan ring and the insanity of our night with The Raven, I might not have believed him. However, the look in Tenny's eyes gave me no doubt that he was telling the truth.

Tenny continued down the street past the alligator creature and saw yet another disturbing thing. In the shadows outside of another shop was a naked couple making love. Out in the wide open on the side walk and in the middle of the night. He was shocked and said he had never seen such a greasy thing in his life. He sprinted away as fast as he could.

It makes me wonder what the Fallbrook police are up to during the night. Are Tenny and I the only people seeing all these crazy things? Does the regular Fallbrook populace know something I do not? Perhaps the police are actually behind it all, I do not know yet. Hopefully they don't arrest me or toss me in the asylum for conspiracy. If you still do not believe me or the accounts of Tenny, I dare you to walk the streets of Fallbrook after midnight. Tell me what you see.

After these disturbing sights through downtown, Tenny turned towards the Mission Road hill. He was now following the same route that I used to take. The smell of burning pipes grew stronger in the air, but Tenny fearlessly kept jogging. He told me that he did not see anything else, but said it felt like he was being watched for the remainder of the jog.

As Tenny ran back up the final stretch of road towards the Studio, emergency vehicles were parked with their lights flashing. Tenny feared for the worst. He thought I had fallen asleep at the wheel or the Raven had caused me to crash. Frantically jogging to the nearest officer, he asked what had happened. The officer said they received a call about a fire, but the whole thing was apparently a "false alarm." Tenny trotted onward.

The Mustang was waiting right where he left it. Tenny's intestines had apparently brewed up quite a storm during his jog, because he had to poop so bad that he could not wait for me to return. He opened the Mustang door to improvise as a bathroom stall, and pooped right there on the curb. Not having any toilet paper, he took his underwear off and wiped with them. Tenny was not about to stink up his own car, so he tossed the soiled undies over the fence into some poor stranger's backyard. He quickly pulled his pants up as someone was walking up the street towards him.

I'm not sure how true this next detail is, but I will tell you anyways. The person who was walking up the street was one of our neighbors, and they made a comment to Tenny about a foul stench in the air. Tenny simply smiled and said "The sewer is leaking." I really can't believe some of the things that my brother does.

Back on the 5.

The Raven looked so adorable in the passenger seat, like a full-sized sleeping baby. She even made sweet little noises and squeezed her hands in the air. It was like her brain had died in the studio and she was slowly coming back to life in the Jeep. Drool began to roll down her cheek but I did not want to wipe it and awaken her. After what felt like hours, we were back in San Juan Capistrano.

I pulled into a dark corner behind the Shell station and parked the Jeep. Exhaustion was overwhelming me, I needed to get some rest before I could deliver the Raven back to her nest. Moments after I closed my eyes I heard a noise. It was a skateboarder rolling past, with a perfectly stuffed backpack that I imagine he lived out of. Maybe he was a professional skater or freelance videographer. Perhaps he was homeless because he wanted to be. What a life he must live, a life I would like to try myself someday. I closed my eyes and slept a few more minutes.

Then I awoke to another noise. This time it was the Raven. She had awoken from her slumber and began speaking to me in slow motion. "Soooooooooooooooooo, helllllllllllooooooooo?" were her first words. I must admit I was quite shocked. I responded, "Yes. Hello." What she said next was unintelligible gibberish and I raised my eyebrows. After a moment of awkward silence, I opened the memo app on my phone and handed it to her. Her eyes lit up and she said "Memo?" I was tired and losing patience. I took the phone back and typed in "Should I call someone?" I returned the phone to her where she slowly read what I had typed.

It was like the world's first computer processor. After sounding out what I typed, she exclaimed "Yes!" and began to type a number slower than I knew was possible. I'm not sure if you've seen the movie Zootopia, but it was like the Sloth's at the DMV. If you haven't seen Zootopia, go rent it once you finish reading this.

She typed a number into my phone but spoke a different number out loud. I dialed the number she announced, but got no response. I then tried the number she had typed, again no response. She gave me a sad look. Then out of nowhere and in plain English, she asked "Is there a bathroom nearby?"

I was beyond confused, and somewhat annoyed, but said yes and pointed towards the gas station. Her next question was "Go with me?" I nodded, got out of the car and opened her door. She unbuckled her seatbelt and got out of the Jeep under her own power. I was expecting her to face plant once more, but she held her ground just fine. At this point she looked down and saw the camouflage Crocs on her feet. She seemed confused, then looked up and saw the Shell sign. She asked, "Are we near home?" I told her we were about a mile and a half away. She said "Let's go."

I agreed and was relieved that I didn't have to deal with any potential drama at the gas station. She climbed back into the Jeep and buckled up. I climbed in and started my phone's navigation, then started the engine. As we pulled out of the gas station and got back on the 74 she waved goodbye to the Shell sign. Every street sign we passed she read aloud, knowing that we were getting closer and closer to the nest.

I made the sharp turn into the neighborhood. "Drive like your kids live here," she told me. I laughed and thought to myself "If I had kids they wouldn't live here." I slowly pulled into the driveway and shut off the Jeep. Looking at her I asked if I was allowed to come inside, she said "Yes."

I got out and opened her door. Remaining in her seat, she asked me "What's the story?" After a pausing for a moment, I said, "My brother and I had a fight, so I left and took you home." She said OK. I just wished all this madness to be over so I could go and sleep.

It did not appear like she remembered anything about the night. She looked around the Jeep for a moment, and realized her phone, jacket, and crazy shoes were gone. I promised I would return them to her. She smiled and gave me a hug before we walked towards the front door. Outside the door was a mountain of boxes that looked like they had been sitting for quite a long time. Strange I thought, but went to knock anyways.

It took 3 tries before her mother answered. I was shocked at the utter lack of concern this woman had for her offspring. I know my own mother would have been frantic on the streets and calling 911 if I were missing. Not this woman. I could have kidnapped her daughter and she probably wouldn't have cared, maybe I would have even been doing her a favor.

At last, the Raven's mother answered the door. She was a large, hideous woman who I could not believe was the mother of my newly reborn Angel. I told her that my brother and I had fought, so I brought her daughter home for her protection. The troll mother smiled and said "Thank you" in an aged, smoke tainted voice. The Raven went inside and hugged her mother. I glimpsed past the two of them and was disturbed at what I saw.

The house was completely fake on the outside. Inside it was just one floor with massive, cavernous ceilings. The walls were all painted a dark shade of greenish black, and large mirrors were everywhere. I couldn't stop staring. The Raven reminded me to bring her stuff back, snapping me out of my trance. I said I would see her later that day, and quickly turned around heading back towards the car. I got in the Jeep and left.

As I pulled out of the neighborhood and back onto the 74, I couldn't help but scream at the top of my lungs. I was so mind boggled over the events that just took place that I needed to pull over at the Shell station and pause for a moment. I saw the missed call notifications from Tenny, and decided it was time I checked on him.

The phone rang, and he answered breathing heavily. I told him I was alive and asked where he was at. He responded very angrily and loudly "ON THE STREET!" I now realized why he was so angry. In my rush to get the Raven out of the studio and into my car, I had locked him out by mistake. Tenny had been locked out for nearly 3 hours, and his car keys were inside. My mistake. In my defense he never sent a text after failing to call multiple times. If you're reading this brother, I would like to say sorry one more time. I told him I would head back to the studio immediately.

Half way back Tenny called to hurry me up, but I told him I was not going to speed. He said he was about to poop on the doorstep and kick the door down. I hung up and increased my speed. This call repeated itself 2 more times until I finally made it back to the Studio. I parked and looked around, but Tenny was nowhere to be seen. I walked down the path towards the door and saw it remained intact. There was no poop on the welcome mat either. I unlocked the studio and went inside, heading straight to the bathroom to release my full bladder. When I came out of the bathroom, Tenny was standing in the doorway. I smiled and said "I'm back!" He did not seem amused. In fact, he did not say a word. He got a beer from the fridge, and laid on the couch. I decided I would leave him alone for the night.

As I turned the lights off and made ready for bed, Tenny said "We need to talk." I was not particularly in the mood for conversation, but agreed to do so. "How could you leave me locked outside for hours to be with a stupid girl?!" I told him it was not as it seemed. "You don't understand, she died and was reborn in the car!" I realize now that this sounds like complete madness, but it was the truth. Tenny did not understand.

He was convinced the Raven was just a making a scene and acted the whole thing. I knew that was not the case. No amount of reasoning could convince Tenny, so I finally said goodnight. He got up to make a peanut butter and jelly sandwich, and said "This isn't over." I said it was for tonight.

He licked the knife and began twirling it around in his hand, giving me a sinister look. I slowly backed away from him towards my bed, not breaking eye contact. I said "See you tomorrow," as I maneuvered into the corner of the bed where my 12 gauge was secretly stashed. Tenny put the knife down and grabbed his sandwich before returning to the couch. I do not think my brother would actually try to murder me, but it certainly appeared like he wanted to. He definitely could have if he wanted to, but our friendship is simply too great. Had he actually made a move, I do not know if I possess the mental strength to pull the trigger on my own brother. Seeing a gaping hole in him would scar me for life, and I do not think I would be able to live with myself.

After a few minutes of silence, I felt confident that Tenny was no longer a threat. I put my headphones in and pulled out my phone. I went to my music and pressed "Shuffle All." Now, I would like you to know how many songs are on my music playlist. It is over 1,700 songs. Out of all 1,700 choices my phone had to choose from, it decided to play "How Long Will They Mourn Me" by 2Pac.

This is one of my favorite songs, as it reminds me of so many good memories with my brothers and sisters. Particularly with Tenny. Who, moments ago, appeared like he was about to murder me. He had never done such a thing before, in fact he has never even hit me. I wondered if it was the Raven that brought him to almost murdering me. Had she corrupted him? Had she corrupted me?

After these thoughts went through my head I opened up the memo app on my phone to remember the events of the day. The short text conversation from earlier with the Raven was still there, haunting me. I backspaced the entire memo, and then began typing what was to become the story that you are now reading.

I recollected the events of that night, and began connecting the dots from previous events to my encounter with the Raven. I was frightened. I felt as if she was in the room with me once more, staring at me. I got up and went to the restroom, turned the light on and sat on the toilet. I had no intentions of using the toilet, but once I sat down I could feel my bowels rumbling, and soon explosive diarrhea erupted into the toilet. I was disgusted with myself and gave a courtesy flush. More diarrhea commenced. After being certain nothing else remained inside, I flushed once more. I wiped clean and gave a third and final flush.

I felt dirty after unleashing such horror upon the toilet, and wished to be clean. After washing my hands with soap and hot water, I turned the shower on and let the water warm up. I shed my clothes and hopped in, and proceeded to cleanse myself for the next 20 minutes. It's times like these where I like to sleep naked, but with Tenny in the other room in an unpredictable state of mind, I decided some shorts would be best. I laid down and wrapped myself in my incredibly soft 90x90" blanket from Wal-Mart, and entered hibernation.

I did not wake up until 11:45am.

When I woke up Tenny was gone, and I saw he had made no effort to clean up after himself. Dirty paper plates were everywhere and the living room was scattered with his empty beer cans from the night before. I was irritated, but at least he did not murder me in my slumber. I picked up my phone and tried to call him, but he did not answer. Then I sent him a text asking where he was at, but that also went unanswered.

After having a bowl of cereal, I began the daunting task of cleaning up the studio and the mess from the night before. Trash littered the ground and food scraps stained the walls. Dishes were piled sky high in the kitchen sink. The couch cushions were tossed around wildly and still moist from the Raven's seizure spill. Then I saw it. The Raven's phone. The wretched device which was apparently her only lifeline into modern society.

The notification light was flashing constantly with missed messages. I tried to use the phone, but the Raven kept a strange musical lock on it which I could not figure out. It was no matter. I continued cleaning the mess, where I found her crazy shoes and her jacket which also needed to be returned to the nest. I placed the three of them together on the end of the couch in a little formation so that I would not lose track of them. It was such an unusual sight that I had to take a photo of it, which you may have seen on the cover.

The studio was not clean yet, but I could not clean any longer. It was as if the trio was stopping me, demanding I return them to their master. I picked them up and put them on the passenger seat of the Jeep.

I thought about the task at hand, and felt worried. What if the Raven was waiting to ambush me? I had so many other things to do today, why not just forget about her stuff? No. My instincts were telling me that it had to be done. I gathered anything I could potentially need: food, water, and a phone charger. A gun wouldn't be a bad idea either. The Jeep was waiting for me.

As I drove along the 5 back towards San Luis Capistrano, I felt rushed, yet I had not promised the Raven that I would return at any particular time. I just wished to be free from this burden, and it felt like the longest 48 miles of my life. Along the way I debated casting them out the window, but being cursed for a lifetime seemed worse than wasting my gas. At last the exit to the 74 arrived.

The amazing Shell station seemed so normal to me now, like a safe haven, and I pulled in to fuel up. The Jeep's fuel gauge read close to half, but this strange feeling inside me told me I needed to be ready to drive. Far. In fact, this feeling was telling me I should not even speak to the Raven when I returned her things, nor should I loiter in the area any longer. I devised a plan. I was going to make the return a quick, and silent delivery.

I left the station and proceeded towards the neighborhood. As I squealed around the sharp right turn I turned my music off and rolled down the windows. I was getting more and more anxious and could feel adrenaline pumping. My veins appeared like they were on the brink of bursting through my skin. The Raven was not going to catch me.

After backing into the driveway I got out and left the Jeep running. I gathered up her things and ran to the front door. The stack of unopened delivery boxes remained outside the door, so I added the Raven's belongings to the pile. Two quick presses were applied to the doorbell before several loud and frantic knocks were given to the door. The neighbors must have been able to hear that knocking. I did not wait for an answer, instead sprinting back to the Jeep and speeding out of the neighborhood.

My heart nearly pounded out of my chest as I continued down the 74 and onto the 5. The drop off was successful. I took the first exit off the 5 and pulled over to catch my breath and release a scream of relief.

After a few moments of deep breathing, I was startled once more by my phone ringing. It was Tenny. He said he had left at 8:45 in the morning and I was out cold when he left. I didn't remember hearing a thing. He said he had been riding his dirt bike the last few hours which was why he didn't answer the phone earlier. To my relief, he told me that we were still cool even after last night. I knew it would take a lot more than just a crazy girl to break our brotherhood.

Perhaps it wasn't just a girl that caused us to fight. Perhaps, inside that beautiful girl was actually something else. A demon maybe. Possibly even Satan himself, there is no way to know. I will refer to it as the Raven for the rest of my life, so as not to provoke it by mistakenly speaking its actual name.

The events that have occurred since the VHS tape have changed me forever. I am not normally a person to share a lot of things on Facebook or tell everyone and their mother my opinions. I wrote this book as a warning, because the events that happened to me are not just coincidence. I wanted to share this warning with others, and you should do the same for the people you care about.

I did not wish to be known by my real name any longer. The Raven could hunt me down using that name, despite me blocking her phone number and on the Internet. So after returning her things, sitting on the side of the 5, I came up with my new alias. Mud.

I have a love for mud; the inside and outside of the Jeep will show that to be a fact. There is nothing more fun to me than splashing through a freshly created mud hole on a hot summer day. I am proud of the mud on my car and haven't washed it off in nearly a year. The rain cleans it for me every once in awhile. Don't worry, I still clean the interior and take care of all the maintenance on my baby.

I wanted a way to show my new name, and proceeded to do some research on my phone. After a few minutes I saw a "Lids" store was not too far away from my current location on the side of the freeway. I drove to the mall which turned out to be in a very high end area where people drove all these fancy cars. The Jeep looked rather out of place.

I went into the Lids store and gave my request to the nice man at the counter. He said it would be ready in just 20 minutes. While I was wandering around the mall killing time, I saw a Jamba Juice. I haven't had that since I lived in Auburn, so I decided to try their new watermelon smoothie creation. It was possibly the best thing I've ever tasted. While I enjoyed my drink, I continued to write this book and watched the funny pests do their shopping.

Before I knew it, over 30 minutes had passed by and it was time to pick up my hat. It is black with three cursive letters on it written in plain white. Mud. My new alias was complete. Now it was time to begin my work.

I believe everything in life happens for a reason. The spirit of Burton, the spirit of John, and the spirit of the Rock from Lake Henshaw have all been signs of something coming. I just never knew what exactly. I like to think my father is watching me from Heaven, as my Guardian Angel, protecting me from any spirits or demons who come after me like the Raven. He has been watching me from above for the last 8 years, and no serious harm has come to me yet. I know someday I will join him, and be there to watch out for my sister Laurel or my children if I have any.

I have plans to someday return to the locations where I have encountered each of the Spirits, and see if I may be able to communicate with them once again. I do not know if I will ever be ready to return to the Nest. There is something dangerous and far beyond my capabilities going on inside there. Perhaps I will be able to assemble a team to tackle this mission with me. We can go through the portal. We can stop whatever evil phenomenon is going on inside the nest. Perhaps it will be one of you reading this.

I realize now what John really was. He was certainly real as Tenny, Brandon, Marcus and myself had all seen him, and Brandon and I talked to him. When we all got up and walked to the picnic table, he *did* vanish. It is likely a power that certain creatures possess, possibly including the Raven. He could even be the same kind of creature as the Raven. Portrayed as a normal human on the outside but something completely different within.

It is possible that male Ravens are less savage than the female variety, but equally as intelligent. The females seem to possess a deceptive quality that is likely how they gather their prey. Perhaps the Raven had young inside her nest and wished to lure me inside to feed them. The "friend" who she was constantly talking to could have even been the father. I will never know. I always stick with my gut feeling, and it told me not to go inside when she invited me in.

I may study the nest from a safe distance using technology and teamwork, but it will require careful planning. I believe I can reacquire the Raven on the internet once more and study her using my different alias. She will not catch me off guard the next time I encounter her.

My whole life I have felt this strange power within me. That I'm not just another ordinary pest. That I am a different kind of creature, perhaps I am even a Raven and just never realized it. Perhaps I have powers that have not been unlocked yet.

No, Ravens are a different breed altogether. I am a Raven Hunter, seeking them out from amongst the rest of the pests and putting them under the spotlight. Maybe my father's sudden demise was the result of a Raven, and it is my destiny to avenge him. The Sprinter van that followed Tenny and me could have been other Raven Hunters, keeping a close eye on us while we escorted the Raven around. I hope to see them again someday and possibly join forces.

I will be out traveling the world on a quest to find more Ravens by the time you are reading this. Be wary. Know that if you do not hear from me within 9 months that the Ravens have swooped me up and I am likely dead or worse. If that is the case, please remember Mud and what I have done. John and the Raven are the only two of their kind that I have ever encountered in my life so far, and I know they will not be the last. The VHS may offer some insight on what I have experienced, but it is something that truly cannot be described without seeing it in person.

I fear what the next Raven may turn out to be like, as it may be more powerful than anything yet. I advise all of you reading this to be ready for it. Expect the unexpected, and watch for the signs that might be right before your eyes. You may have noticed the several * scattered throughout this book. What do you think they mean?

I will tell you what they meant to me. I saw them as omens, warning signs of what was to come. This book may have never been written had I not paid more attention to them. More unnatural events than the ones I described to you have occurred, but that will be another story. On a side note, if you have made it this far into my mind I ask something of you. Please give me some input on any grammatical errors you think exist so that future generations don't have to see them. Thank you. Before I bid you farewell and you continue on with your day, I ask you two questions. What is the password and what is the lock? Goodbye.

MUD

ABOUT THE AUTHOR

Mud is the creator of Shower Thoughts Studios.

A collection of Reading, Writing, Recording, and Listening. The Studio is comprised of four friends who share an unbreakable bond, created from years of shared hardship. We all come from very different places, but work together as one. Lost Minds, a modern rap duo, records from the Studio and will be releasing an album in the future. Mud also has plans for a second book as well as a movie, but both are in the very early stages at this time.

 Gorilla Girl Ink is the publishing company of Mud's grandmother. She is an English professor and the author of the Hillary Broome Novels. Contact her at www.junegillam.com